Betrayed by her own mother . . .

"Thanks for your offer, honey," my mom said, "but I don't think I'll need your help this time. Not for the show itself, that is. You can help get the store ready, maybe set up chairs. But too many people running around at the show would just create confusion."

"I wouldn't be too many people," I said.

"Well, Lucienne is bringing a crew with her, and of course I'll have Nicole. I don't think we'll need any more help than that."

I couldn't believe it. I—who had given her great advice on what to stock at Cinderella, who read every fashion magazine published, who had wanted to meet Lucienne ever since I first saw her designs—I would be setting up chairs while Nicole Barker worked on the show. Life was not fair.

Ask your bookseller for these other PARTY LINE titles:

Special party tips in every book!

ROSIE'S FASHION SHOW

by Carrie Austen

SPLASH™

A BERKLEY / SPLASH BOOK

THE PARTY LINE #12: ROSIE'S FASHION SHOW is an original publication of The Berkley Publishing Group. This work has never appeared before in book form.

A Berkley Book / published by arrangement with General Licensing Company, Inc.

PRINTING HISTORY
Berkley edition / April 1991

ISBN: 0-425-12652-8
RL: 6.0

A BERKLEY BOOK® TM 757,375
Berkley Books are published by The Berkley Publishing Group, 200 Madison Avenue, New York, New York 10016.
The name "BERKLEY" and the "B" logo are trademarks belonging to Berkley Publishing Corporation.

PRINTED IN THE UNITED STATES OF AMERICA

10 9 8 7 6 5 4 3 2 1

ROSIE'S FASHION SHOW

One

As I ran across the park I could see that the side door of the Moondance Café was open, so I ignored the front entrance and ran up the brick walk on the side.

I reached down and grabbed my right sneaker and yanked it off and leapt up to the second step. I got the left sneaker off, then stepped over the third step and into the dining room in my socks. I almost collided with David Bartlett, who was dragging a mop across the floor.

"Hey, Rosie, why are you sneaking around?"

I held up my muddy shoes. "I'm not sneaking. I'm in a hurry and I didn't want to track in mud, so I just took them off."

"There's a doormat on the front porch." David sounded a little grumpy.

"I know, but the side door was closer." I started to move around him.

"Whoa." David leaned on the mop handle, blocking my path.

"David, come on. I'm late already."

"I know. The potato chips and dip went up half an hour ago."

I started to move and David pointed to the end of the dining room. "Go around the edge," he said. "The floor is still wet in the middle."

I ran around the tables and toward the broad staircase.

"Give my regards to the Joint Chiefs of Staff," David yelled as I ran up the steps. "Today they sound more like the Joint Chiefs of Laughs."

I didn't bother to reply, but that last remark made me happy. It meant my friends were in a good mood.

Normally I'm nicer to David, even when he is sarcastic about The Party Line. I mean, he *is* the brother of one of my best friends, Becky, and the Moondance Café is his home. The Moondance is the restaurant that Becky's mother and stepfather run on the first floor of their Victorian house. Actually, right now they're in the process of turning the rest of the house into an inn and moving to a beautiful colonial house across the way. In spite of all the reshuffling, they still let Becky use the attic on the third floor as a meeting place for her friends and her business partners. Yes, Becky has business partners—the entire Party Line. In fact, her very best friends and The Party Line are one and the same: Julie Berger, Allison Gray, and me, Rosie Torres.

That day, Sunday, was the weekly meeting of The Party Line, and I was late. That wasn't a big deal, but I had some really important news and I couldn't wait to tell my friends.

I took the attic stairs two at a time. When I got to the top I saw my friends deeply involved with a bowl of potato chips.

"Hi, guys, " I panted. "You're not going to believe this."

"Rosie, unless the Moondance is on fire, sit down and catch your breath." Becky tossed a pillow at my feet.

I dropped down and blew out a long breath. "I jogged over."

"My grandmother says bad news travels fast," Allie said, sounding a little worried.

I laughed. "My news is totally great, Allie," I said. "Lucienne is coming to Canfield."

Allie smiled. "Lucienne!"

"Not *your* Lucienne?" Becky said.

I nodded.

"That's fantastic, Rosie," Julie said. "I mean, it isn't Roger Clemens, but it's really exciting."

I knew Julie was teasing me, but I gave an exaggerated sigh. "Julie, when are you going to pay attention to the really important things in life?"

Julie mimicked my sigh, then the two of us started laughing. I think it's true about opposites attracting each other. Julie absolutely loves baseball and she can spend hours pouring over a copy of *Sports Illustrated*, while I lose myself in every issue of *Saucy*, my favorite fashion magazine. But as different as we are, Julie is my best friend in the world.

Becky shook her head at Allie. "Do you think they'll recover, or do we have to run The Party Line with two perfectly normal people and two laughing hyenas?"

Julie sat up and saluted Becky. "Sorry, Madam

President. I was overcome by our good friend's news."

"I know exactly how you feel, Rosie," Allie said. "Remember how excited I was when Vermilion sang at Taylor College?" Vermilion is Allie's favorite singer. She's her role model, too, because Allie wants to be a singer herself someday. Ever since she actually got to meet Vermilion after her concert here, Allie's been a lot more confident about her singing. She even made it to the finals of the talent show sponsored by the local TV station!

"I understand that Rosie's excited," Becky said. "It's just that we have a party to plan, and it happens to be next week."

"I didn't mean to get us off the track, Becky," I said. "But this is the biggest thing that's ever happened at Cinderella."

"Wait a minute. Lucienne's coming to Cinderella?" Becky yelped. "You didn't say that!"

"How come?" Julie said.

"Will you get to meet her?" Allie asked.

I nodded. My mother has owned and run Cinderella, a boutique on Main Street, since the year Lucienne introduced her first line of clothing.

Mom loved Lucienne's designs from the start and featured her things even before she was famous.

I explained to my friends that that morning, while I was getting ready to come to The Party Line meeting, Mom had gotten a phone call from New York. It was Lucienne, asking my mother if she would host a fashion show at Cinderella. It seems that Lucienne's favorite cause is a children's hospital in New York, and since she had already planned to organize a touring fashion show to introduce her new line, she got the idea to donate the money from the tickets and a percentage of the money from the clothing orders to the children's hospital. Mom was thrilled that Lucienne wanted Cinderella to be the first store on the tour.

Julie had folded her legs in the lotus position and Allie and Becky had sprawled out on pillows while I told them about Lucienne's plan.

"Wow, Rosie," Allie said. "It must be like a dream come true. I hope you get a chance to show Lucienne some of your own designs."

"I don't know. I've never really designed anything," I said, knowing it wasn't really true. I took my own designs seriously, but I was afraid to show them to someone as amazing as Lucienne. What if she thought they were really childish? What if she even laughed at me? I caught my friends staring at me disbelievingly and plunged on. "I mean, I don't design whole wardrobes of dresses and separates, like Lucienne does," I said lamely. "I just fool around."

"Come on, Rosie," Becky said. "You can do more with a couple of scarves than any designer I've ever seen."

"You really do have a great eye, Rosie," Allie said.

I grinned at her. "My mom said she knew I had an eye for color when I got my first box of crayons and promptly scribbled all over my walls."

"If that's what it takes, Mouse will be a great artist, too," Allie giggled.

Mouse is what we all call Allie's baby brother, Jonathan. He will always have special significance for The Party Line. It was at his fourth-birthday party that The Party Line really began. The clown who was supposed to entertain the kids got sick and Becky, Julie, Allie, and I stepped in and saved the day. Word got out and we started getting calls to give parties for other kids. Becky had the idea of making it a regular business. We all loved the idea and elected her president. Allie is the vice president, I'm the treasurer and, because she has the best handwriting, Julie is the secretary.

"I think it's fate." Julie waved her pencil in the air like a magic wand. "Lucienne coming to Cinderella and Cinderella's owner's daughter being a clothes genius."

"Fate," Becky said, waving her hand slowly in front of Julie's face, as if she were trying to get Julie to snap out of some kind of trance. "Julie, you sound like your sister."

"Becky," Julie said patiently, "Laurel is the horoscope freak. I'm just saying that I think this will be a great opportunity for Rosie to talk shop with her idol. Heck. Lucienne's more than that, even. She's the world's greatest designer!"

"I don't think the world's greatest designer will exactly want to talk shop with me, Julie," I demurred.

"Why not? You may not be a famous designer, but you've got great ideas."

"I've got great friends," I said, laughing.

"Now, about this meeting," Becky said.

"Yeah, Becky," Julie said with mock impatience. "Why don't you call this meeting to order? Don't you know we've got party business?"

"Oh, is that why we're here?" Becky asked.

Allie and I giggled at the faces Becky and Julie made at each other.

"Wait," Julie said. "Before we get too busy, the secretary has a request."

"Yes, esteemed secretary?" Becky said.

"I request you pass those potato chips to me right away."

"Now," Becky said, sitting back on her cushion, "the meeting will come to order and Allie will tell us about the party."

"It's for Belinda Collins. Her sister Francie was at Ellie Turner's party and recommended us to her mom."

Becky frowned. "Ellie Turner?"

"Remember? When Julie had her broken leg?" Allie prompted.

Julie groaned. "Oh no, I absolutely refuse to break my leg again. I don't care how much Francie liked it."

Allie threw a pillow at Julie. "You nut. Francie loved the balloon animals, not your leg."

The Party Line business meeting was back to normal: half party business, half monkey business. Belinda Collins's birthday was the next Saturday, so the party planning had to be a rush job.

"We need to think of a theme," Becky said. "Do her parents have any particular idea in mind?"

Allie shrugged. "Belinda's mother said it was up to us. She's going to be ten."

"What do ten-year-olds like to do?" Julie asked.

"Think back," Allie said. "It was only three years ago."

"They like the same things we do," I said.

"They probably don't drool over boys the way you and Julie do," Becky said.

Julie laughed and tossed a pillow, which landed squarely on Becky's head.

Julie and I are not boy-crazy. Can we help it if certain members of the opposite sex are irresistibly cute?

We spent the next thirty minutes trading thoughts on what ten-year-olds like, but we didn't come up with any great ideas. Becky finally ended the meeting because it was time for Gemini's dinner. Gemini is the horse Becky bought for a dollar from the Parkers, who used to live in the house that the Bartletts are moving into. Becky's fantastic with Gemini—sometimes it almost seems as if they can read each other's thoughts. Becky's great with all animals, though, so it makes perfect sense that she wants to be a veterinarian when she's older.

"Gonna put on the old feed bag?" Julie asked slyly.

"Gem doesn't eat out of a feed bag, Julie," Becky replied very seriously. "She has a feed trough. You know that."

"Of course I do. It's just a figure of speech," Julie retorted. "Besides, I think a feed bag is a great idea. You just hook it on and they can walk around while they eat."

"Like you at the mall," I said.

Julie almost fell apart laughing at that. It's a well-known fact that Julie eats everything in sight and never gains an ounce. She never takes offense at the mention of her appetite, either.

Julie's good humor was infectious and Allie and I started laughing. Becky is smart enough to know that when the giggles hit, no more business gets done, so she ended the meeting.

"Okay everybody, do some thinking," Becky said, closing the door behind her as we all trooped down the hall. "If anyone gets a good party idea, start up the telephone chain."

The phone chain is our system for keeping in touch with one another without having to make lots of phone calls. For example, if I have some news, instead of making three calls I just call Julie, who calls Allie, who calls Becky. We try to make the calls as close to eight o'clock as we can. That makes our parents happy. It also works well for Julie, who has two older sisters who are practically welded to the phone, and for Allie, who has four brothers and sisters.

Becky headed for the stable while Allie, Julie, and I went out the side door. Julie unlocked her bike and began walking it down the sidewalk beside Allie and me.

"I feel like my brain is in neutral," Allie said. "I just can't think of anything for Belinda's party."

"I know how you feel," I said. "My thoughts keep wandering back to Lucienne and the fashion show."

"It's because it's so gorgeous out," Julie said.

"Sitting inside on a day like this turns my brain to oatmeal."

"Oatmeal?" Allie laughed. "Leave it to you to bring food into it, Julie."

"Speaking of the great outdoors, Julie," I said. "When I came through the park I saw Mark Harris and some of the guys from school at the baseball field."

Julie has a mega-crush on Mark. "Were they playing?" she asked.

"I guess. Casey Wyatt was dumping a duffel full of bats and balls on the ground."

"Great." Julie's eyes lit up. "You guys mind if I take off?"

"It's okay, Julie," Allie said, "but remember we still have the problem of a party theme."

Julie grinned and swung onto her bike. "For ten-year-olds. I got it." She started pedaling and yelled over her shoulder, "Find a five-year-old and ask her what she likes, then double it!"

Two

Sometimes parents are weird. Take my mom, for instance. She had this huge fashion show coming up, so you'd think she'd want all the help she could get, wouldn't you? And help from someone who knows something. Me, I mean. I'm not a rocket scientist, but I know about clothes. After all, I was brought up with Cinderella, so what would be more natural than for me to help with a fashion show there?

On Sunday afternoon, as I was cleaning out my dresser drawers, I kept thinking about how wonderful it could be. Every piece of clothing I picked up started another daydream. I pictured myself backstage at the fashion show, surrounded by beautiful clothes, helping Lucienne dress the models. I could practically feel the lights and hear the music.

Suddenly Lucienne gasps. She can't find the scarf that goes with her fabulous sage-green silk dress! I whip off my own pumpkin-colored scarf and tie it artfully around the model's waist. It looks stunning, and Lucienne is astonished by my incredibly clever innovation. She says she has never seen anyone with my natural fashion talent, and asks me to work with her for the rest of the tour! Next stop: Paris!

I folded my pumpkin-colored scarf and put it in the drawer just as Mom called me to come downstairs. I hoped for about the twelfth time that afternoon that she would ask me to work on the show. Instead she asked me to set the table.

I finally decided it was time to drop a few small hints about what a help I could be. I reminded her about the great window displays I'd done for Cinderella. I reminded her of the great makeover I'd done on Jennifer Peterson. I even reminded her of what I had done to my walls with my first box of crayons.

Do you think my mom noticed? No way. The hints got as big as elephants. But not only didn't she notice, she acted as if I weren't even there.

Well, not quite. She reminded me to make my bed and to practice for my piano lesson.

After school on Monday I met Allie and Becky by the side door.

"Hi, Rosie," Becky said. "Have you seen Julie? I want to walk home so we can talk about Belinda's party."

I shook my head. "I have to take the bus today. My piano lesson is Thursday and I have to practice. I promised my mom. She thinks I haven't been spending enough time on it lately."

Allie groaned. "Rosie, we need your input. I made a list of all the party themes we've used so far. I thought we could go through it and come up with something for Belinda."

Allie is so organized. She says it's the only way to survive when you're a member of a big family. But I have the feeling that if Allie were shipwrecked on a desert island, the first thing she'd do would be to name all the animals and count all the trees. We're lucky to have her in The Party Line.

"Here, Rosie." Allie handed me a sheet of paper. "I made a copy for each of us."

The sheet had four color-coded columns. The name of the kid who had had the party was in green, the theme in red, the food in blue, and the cost in black.

"This is great, Allie. I'll study it on the bus and call you tonight to see what you guys have come up with."

Becky was looking over her sheet. "Let's see. Why not take the clowns from Mouse's party, the balloon animals from Ellie's, the food from Patti's roller-skating party . . ."

"The bus is leaving. I have to go."

Becky and Allie waved to me as the bus chugged down the drive. I saw Julie run up and the three of them start to walk home. I wished I had stayed with them. Good friends are maybe the most important thing in the world. Nothing would mean as much if I couldn't share it with them—even being a great designer. *Especially* being that, I thought.

I leaned back in my seat and put together my own fashion show. But the models in my show were Allie, Becky, and Julie. I imagined Allie, with her long, wavy brown hair and big blue eyes, in something really romantic, like a fluffy angora sweater over a gauzy skirt. I pictured Becky in a red leather mini and red tights, with tons of bangles on her wrists. I put Julie in soft, white cottons. I was just putting some silver beads on her white sweater when I realized with a jolt that we had reached my stop.

I looked down and saw Allie's list in my hand. I had unconsciously folded and unfolded it so many times, it was practically coming apart. I shoved it in my pocket and grabbed my backpack.

I had finished practicing and was setting the table for dinner when my mom pulled into the driveway. She was carrying a load of stuff in from the car, so I ran out to help.

"Let me give you a hand, Mom."

"Thanks, darling. Be careful with those fabric samples. They're silk."

I carefully took a load of material from her arms. "What's all this?"

"They're the predominant colors in Lucienne's new line. I want to match up some displays in the store to showcase them."

"This purple is awesome."

"It's called aubergine." Mom put down her

stuff, dropped into a chair in the kitchen, and kicked off her shoes. She closed her eyes and rubbed her forehead.

I figured that this would be a perfect time to offer to help with Lucienne's show.

"Mom, the fashion show is a lot of work," I said. "I think I could really—"

"Rosie, not now. I don't want to think about that show for the next fifteen minutes. I want to have a cup of tea and put my feet up."

"I'll get your tea." I put some water on to boil and then sliced a lemon very thin, just the way she likes it. I got out the honey and then finished setting the table.

When she had finished her tea, I asked, "Mom, we don't have anything big coming up at school and The Party Line has only one party, which will be over on Saturday, so I'll be free to help with the fashion show."

"Thanks, honey, but I don't think I'll need you this time. Not for the show itself, that is. You can help get the store ready, but too many people running around that Sunday would just create confusion."

"I wouldn't be too many people," I said.

"Well, Lucienne is bringing people with her, and of course I have Nicole. I don't think we'll need any more help than that."

I quickly turned around and started filling water glasses so my mom couldn't see the tears in my eyes. I couldn't believe that she was choosing Nicole Barker to help her instead of me. Nicole was a seventeen-year-old high-school cheerleader whom Mom hired last year to help out at Cinderella. There is really nothing wrong with Nicole, but I never liked her less than I did at that moment.

I turned on the water full force. "Nicole will be a great help, I'm sure. It only took her a month to figure out how to shake pom-poms."

"Rosie, I can't hear you with that water on," my mother said.

"It wasn't important, Mom." I bit my lip. I was surprised at myself. I don't usually think catty things like that. But I was really upset. I wanted to work on the show more than anything, even more than a date with Ben Barrow.

I was putting the glasses on the table when Mom came over and gave me a quick hug.

"Thanks, honey. I'll tell you what: I'll work out

a schedule for you to help with the preparations for the show. We'll have to clear out the back room and construct some sort of runway. Then there are the chairs . . ."

I couldn't believe it. I—who had given her great advice on what to stock at Cinderella, who kept up with every fashion magazine, who had wanted to meet Lucienne ever since I saw her first designs—I would be setting up chairs while Nicole Barker worked on the show. Life was not fair.

When I was a kid, I loved an old-fashioned book on etiquette my mom has. (It had been her grandmother's.) There's a picture in it of a teary-eyed little boy peeking through a window at a party, where a bunch of kids are eating up a storm. I had felt so sorry for the boy, I drew a big drumstick in his hand. My mom hadn't been too pleased that I had drawn in her book, but she patiently explained that the boy wasn't crying because he was hungry. He was hurt at being left out.

That was exactly how I felt.

At lunch the next day I had no appetite. I took a tuna sandwich, a bag of chips, and an orange juice and headed for the table where Becky and Allie were sitting. Becky had brought a monster roast-beef sandwich from the Moondance. She was sharing it with Allie.

"Hi." I put my tray down. "What's going on?"

"Hi," Becky said. "There's enough of this sandwich for three, if you'd like some."

I shook my head. "Thanks, but I don't even want what I have. I wonder where Julie is?"

Allie pointed. "In line, where else? Today's chili day."

"Oh yeah." I slid into a chair and sighed.

I saw Becky and Allie glance at each other. "Rosie," Becky said, "you look a little gloomy. Are you okay?"

I managed a grin. "I'm sorry. I guess I am a little depressed."

"Depressed?" Julie came up to the table and set her tray next to mine. "What's wrong?"

I told them about what my mother had said when I volunteered to help out with the fashion show.

"Well, Rosie," Allie said, "maybe your mom is nervous about the show because it's her first and she wants . . . uh, grownups working on it."

I shrugged. I didn't want to sound like a jealous little kid, so I didn't mention Nicole. But I didn't have to.

Julie stopped crumbling crackers into her bowl of chili and looked up. "Nicole Barker told Heather that she's going to work on the fashion show." Julie said. Nicole goes to school with Julie's sister Heather. "Boy, is that bogus."

"Is it ever," Becky said. "I'm sure Nicole is fine and everything, but if I had to pick someone to work on a fashion show it would definitely be Rosie."

"Yeah," Allie agreed. "It does seem strange for your mom not to let you work on the show if she's letting Nicole do it. I mean, you've done fantastic window displays for the store and you've even given her great advice on what merchandise to order. She knows what you can do."

"Wait a second, you guys. I know you're trying to help, but this conversation is really bumming me out," I said.

"I'm sorry, Rosie. I didn't mean to do that," Julie said. Allie and Becky nodded, too.

"How about this?" Becky said with a gleam in her eye. "Mouse was just exposed to chickenpox, wasn't he, Allie? We could take him to Cinderella and expose Nicole. She'd be breaking out—oh, I'd say just about the day of the show."

I had to laugh. Becky has the most outrageous ideas sometimes!

"No, that's no good. What if she's already had them?" Julie said. "I say we send Nicole a telegram saying that she's won a trip to Bermuda and that she has to leave on the day of the fashion show."

"I just can't believe my mom chose a girl with the IQ of a cornflake over me," I sniped. I just couldn't help it. It just burst out of me.

There was a moment of silence as Becky, Allie, and Julie exchanged glances.

"Wow, Rosie, that doesn't sound like you," Julie said.

"You must really feel awful, Rosie," Allie said.

"Yeah," I said. "That was really mean. I shouldn't take it out on Nicole just because my mom prefers her to me."

"Come on," Becky said. "You know that's not true."

"It sounds dumb, doesn't it?" I sighed. "I don't think I would feel so bad if it were any other designer who was coming. But *Lucienne!*" I could feel tears pricking my eyelids. I blinked hard. The cafeteria was the last place I wanted to cry.

"Rosie, Allie's right. Your mom's just really stressed out because she's never done this before," Julie said.

"Yeah," Becky said, "you know how parents get. She'll let you work on the next one for sure."

"The next one won't be Lucienne's," I said glumly. I saw my friends exchange glances again.

Then Becky waved her napkin like a handkerchief and put on her best Juliet voice. "What's in a name? That which we call Lucienne by any other name would still be high fashion."

Not long ago Becky had ended up playing the lead in *Romeo and Juliet*. She hadn't wanted to at first, but it turned out she was pretty good as Juliet. Now she was mugging it up while she mangled Shakespeare. She flung her arms wide. The napkin flew out of her hand and floated to the floor.

Becky pushed back her chair, but before she could move to get the napkin from the floor, Casey Wyatt ran over and grabbed it. He wadded it up and tossed it to her.

"Here, Bartlett," he said loudly. "Don't you know it's against the law to be a litterbug?"

Becky dropped the napkin on her tray. Casey had rolled up the soggy core of an apple in it. "Ugh," she said. "He's such a dweeb."

I had to smile in spite of myself. My friends all smiled back and Julie gave my shoulder a very light punch.

"Listen, Rosie," she told me earnestly. "Give your mom time. Any day now she'll wake up and realize that the fashion expert of the century is right there in her own home."

I could only hope my friends were right. Could the power of positive thinking really work?

The lunch bell rang and we all picked up our lunch trays and headed toward the tray return.

"Listen, I'm officially calling a meeting of The Party Line for this afternoon," Becky said. "We've *got* to get going on Belinda's party."

"Okay. See you later," Julie said. "I gotta go brush before class." She pointed to her braces.

"Meet at the side door after school," Becky said as we all juggled our books and headed down the hall.

"Fashion," Allie said suddenly.

Becky and I looked at her. She smiled. "I think I've got it."

"Got what?" I said, but just then the final bell rang and we hurried into history class where Mr. Epstein was already writing a list of major Civil War battles on the board.

Becky sighed. "Great. Now we won't be able to find out what Allie was talking about until after the Civil War."

Three

I don't sit near Allie in history so I couldn't pass her a note, but I did see her slip a note to Julie, who sits right in front of her. I caught up to Julie at the door of English class.

"Rosie, Allie's got a great idea," she said, thumbing through her notebook.

Just then Ms. Lombardi came to the doorway. "Thinking about joining us this afternoon, girls?"

Julie shrugged and whispered, "Later." We went to our seats. I was too curious and distracted to pay much attention in class. I was supposed to be writing an essay, but I started doodling and got carried away. Before long, I realized my doodle had turned into Nicole Barker in a little polka-dot dress a lot like one that Lucienne had featured the season before. It reminded me of Becky's idea to expose Nicole to chickenpox.

I put dots on the figure's face so forcefully that I broke the point on my pencil. I giggled and flipped the page to start writing, but it was too late; a hand tapped me on the shoulder.

"Is there something funny you'd like to share, Rosie?" Ms. Lombardi asked.

I felt my face get hot and was about to try to explain the doodle, but my teacher spoke first.

"Can you stay after class for a few minutes, Rosie? I'd like to put your considerable artistic talent to a *good* use."

"Sure, Ms. Lombardi." I sagged in my seat. She had seen my notebook.

Finally the bell rang. I looked over at Julie, who waved and headed for the hall. I went up to Ms. Lombardi's desk. She looked up and smiled at me. *It was a good start*, I thought.

"Rosie," she said, "I wish I had a talent for drawing like you do. It's a wonderful tool of communication."

I nodded, but inside I was beginning to get really worried. I was sure she was going to ask what I had been trying to communicate with the picture of the polka-dotted girl in my notebook.

Luckily, she surprised me. She didn't even mention my notebook at all. She explained that she taught a special-ed class on Saturdays for hearing-impaired children. She had made a hand puppet, which she called Miss Elf, to use as a teaching tool, and the kids loved it. She wanted me to draw a cartoon of Miss Elf so she could make copies to give to the kids.

Miss Elf was a cute puppet and I saw that I could make a cute cartoon of her. She had a round head with yellow yarn hair, two blue felt stars for eyes, and a red felt mouth. There was a sprinkling of freckles over her little nose. Her mouth came off and could be replaced by a red felt U that made Miss Elf look like she was grinning from ear to ear or, with the U turned upside down, like she was very sad.

"She's adorable, Ms. Lombardi," I said.

"Take as much time as you need," she said. "I know how busy you are with schoolwork and your party business."

"The Party Line," I said. "We have a meeting this afternoon."

"Then I won't keep you any longer."

I said goodbye and headed for the door, breathing a sigh of relief that she had forgotten about my doodle.

"By the way, Rosie," Ms. Lombardi called as I reached the door, "Miss Elf has a few freckles—but not nearly as many as the girl in your notebook."

As I climbed the stairs to Becky's attic that afternoon, I got a funny feeling. I remembered how I had felt the Sunday before when I had been heading for the attic. I remembered how excited I had been about Lucienne coming to Canfield, and how I had thought I was going to get to work with her. I could feel my spirits sag. I caught a look at my face in the big old-fashioned mirror in the attic, and my mouth was sagging, too. For a second I could see the sad-looking Miss Elf.

I didn't want to drag down The Party Line meeting, so I tried a big Miss Elf smile. I looked so silly that I laughed, and was still smiling as my friends came up the attic stairs with their arms full of great Moondance leftovers. "Okay, what is this great idea of Allie's?" I asked.

"Rosie, is this your new exercise program?" Becky said. "Running up the stairs to our meetings?"

"Keep it up," Julie said. "It keeps you thin so you can eat more."

Julie held up a tray. "More delicious munchies, courtesy of the Moondance." There had been a private party the night before and Russell, Becky's stepfather (who does all the restaurant's cooking) had sent up the leftovers for us.

I took a cheese puff and a piece of celery stuffed with some pink goo and flopped down on my favorite red Oriental rug.

Julie popped a stuffed mushroom in her mouth. "Mmm. What do you call these, Becky?"

"Canapés," Becky said.

I sampled the cheese puff. "Delicious. Now, will someone please tell me Allie's idea?"

"Fashion," Allie said.

"Fashion." I groaned. "Rub it in, why don't you?"

"W-wait a s-second, Rosie," Allie said.

"Yeah, let Allie tell you her whole idea," Becky said.

I felt terrible. Allie only stutters when she's

nervous or upset. "I'm sorry, Allie. I guess I've just heard that word too many times lately, and you know how bummed I've been about the Lucienne show. Tell me what you had in mind."

"Well, because you're so great at putting clothes together, and you've done so many great makeovers, I thought it would be fun to do a fashion theme for Belinda's party," Allie explained. "She's going to be ten, and I know from her mother that she's been getting into clothes lately."

"What else should she be getting into?" Julie said, imitating her grandmother, Goldie. "Paper bags, maybe?"

Allie laughed, "She's into clothes the way you're into those stuffed mushrooms."

"I think it's a great idea," Becky said.

"Me, too. What do you think?" Julie asked me.

I smiled to myself. I could tell Allie had thought of this idea to make me feel better, and it did. Even if it didn't seem like my mom appreciated me, I knew my friends did.

"I think it's a great idea," I said. "How about if one of the activities is T-shirt decorating?"

"T-shirts!" Julie said. "That sounds perfect."

"I can get plain white ones wholesale through Cinderella," I said.

"Wholesale, that's great." Allie reached for her notebook.

"The kids will love it," Becky said. "And I saw this fabulous fabric paint on sale at the Wishbone. They have the sparkly kind in every color imaginable."

I nodded. "I've got some tubes of that at home, and there's boxes of stuff in the back room at Cinderella, like buttons, sequins, ribbons, and other neat stuff. We'll be doing my mom a favor by taking it because she wants the place cleaned out before . . . you know."

Allie looked up from her notebook, where she had been writing. "Before what?" she asked.

"Lucienne's fashion show," Becky and Julie said at the same time.

"Oh, yeah," Allie said. "I almost forgot about that."

I laughed. "You know, I forgot about it for a while myself. Pass me another canapé, Becky."

As we pigged out on the luscious leftovers, the ideas kept coming. We all agreed that cheese puffs and stuffed mushrooms must be brain food, because the more we ate, the better the ideas got.

I had an idea for a game that would fit in with the clothing theme. It was simple and didn't require much equipment. We only had to find pictures of clothing, the funnier the better. When a guest arrived we would pin a picture on the back of her shirt so that she couldn't see it but everyone else could. Each guest would ask the other girls questions about the picture on her back, such as, "Is it worn mostly by women or is it usually worn by men?" The first one to guess what her picture was would win.

Everyone had ideas about what the pictures should be. Becky suggested a fifties poodle skirt and Allie liked the idea of men's long johns. We decided that we would have to give some thought as to what would be the most fun for ten-year-olds.

"We'll all bring pictures that we think we can use in the game and we'll sort them out on Friday," Becky said in her most presidential manner.

"So we'll start with the game, then we'll decorate the T-shirts. I could give each guest a mini-makeover, and we'll end with a little fashion show," I said. "So they can show off their T-shirt creations."

We all agreed and went on to deciding about the food. I was surprised at how enthusiastic I had gotten about the party, especially considering how depressed I'd felt when I arrived.

"If we're going to have the kids working with T-shirts, paints, and glue," I said, "we should keep the food simple."

"Good thought," Allie said. She was making a list of the supplies we'd need.

"Let's just set out bowls of colorful candy, like Gummi Bears and M&Ms and licorice," Becky suggested. "Then we'll have ice cream, cake, and soda when they're done creating their fashion statements."

We ran out of party ideas just about the time we ran out of food. Funny coincidence, huh? We cleaned up the remnants of the snacks and agreed that we'd do the shopping Friday after school.

When I got home, I worked on the cartoon of Miss Elf for Ms. Lombardi. I gave the puppet a big smile.

I showed Mom the picture when it was finished.

I guess I secretly wanted to remind her of my artistic talents. She was delighted with Miss Elf. In fact, she was in such a good mood about everything that I decided to ask her again about working on the fashion show. Then the phone rang. When she hung up she told me she had to go back to the store to deal with some fashion-show emergency. She said goodbye and ran out the door.

I had never felt so ignored by my mother. Lucienne's show, which a few days earlier had seemed like a dream come true, was beginning to seem more like a nightmare. I took my pencil and changed Miss Elf's smile to a big frown—to match my own.

Four

We walked to the Pine Tree Mall on Friday afternoon to do the party shopping. Allie and Becky were in front of Julie and me. All the way there my friends talked about the different ideas they had for T-shirt designs. I made a few half-hearted suggestions, even though I really wasn't in the mood to talk about anything that had to do with clothes designing.

"You feel okay, Rosie?" Julie asked.

"Sure, why?"

"The last time you were so quiet, you ended up in the hospital. They got rid of your tonsils then, though, so I know that can't be the problem."

She was referring to my tonsillectomy a few months earlier. For two days I had tried to wish my sore throat away, and had hardly said a word, but eventually I'd had to face up to the fact that I needed surgery.

The whole experience was kind of scary—especially since I'm a big baby when it comes to any kind of pain—but in a weird way I'm glad it happened, because while I was in the hospital I met Skye Friedman, a girl our age. She had been in the hospital for experimental open-heart surgery, which was completely successful. I'd visited her a few times since then, and she was having a great time doing all the things, such as sports, that she'd never been able to do before the surgery.

"Hey, guys," said Becky, turning around. I was happy for the interruption. I didn't want to tell Julie how I was really feeling, but I couldn't lie to her, either.

"I forgot to tell you that I ordered the cake from Matthew," she said. Matthew, who does the baking for the Moondance, also does all The Party Line's cakes. Not only is he the best baker in town, he's also the most creative. Plus he gives us a terrific discount.

"I told him about the fashion theme," Becky

went on. "He thought it sounded like fun. He said he'd come up with a special cake."

"Like what?" Allie asked.

"He wouldn't tell me," Becky said. "He just said 'trust me.'"

"What'll we do first?" Becky asked as we entered the main doors of the mall. She looked over at me. Usually I want to stop by Winter's cosmetic counter to check out the new makeup. "Rosie, are you up for a makeover?"

"On who?" I asked.

"I could use some lip gloss," Allie said.

"I thought maybe you could help me pick out a good blush," said Becky, who almost never wore makeup.

I knew they were saying that just for me. Doing makeovers is one of my favorite things. "I don't think we'll have time," I said. "Remember, we have to stop by Cinderella on our way home to pick up the stuff from the back room." We decided to head straight for The Perfect Party.

"I hope we have time to try out that new pizza place," Julie said. "We should hit it early so we don't spoil our dinners."

"Has anything ever spoiled your dinner?" Allie asked.

Becky sighed, then took charge as a president should. "Okay, we'll get the party stuff first, then pizza. Last stop here will be at Sew and Sew to pick up the fabric glue and stuff. Then we go on to Cinderella for T-shirts and decorating supplies."

We all nodded, though Julie couldn't resist pointing out that her stomach was already growling.

We found the perfect plates and napkins at The Perfect Party. The plates were white with bright primary-color cartoon drawings of kids playing dress-up.

Allie held up the package. One of the plates depicted a little girl wearing an Egyptian headdress that was sliding off her head. She was holding a worm in her hand. I guessed it was supposed to be some kind of kiddie version of Cleopatra. It was kind of funny that they used a little girl and a worm instead of the grown-up woman with a snake.

"It's what's-her-name." Julie is not a history whiz.

"That's right, Julie, it's old what's-her-name," Allie said.

"It's that Irish girl, Clee O'Patrick," Becky offered.

That's when it happened. The giggle epidemic. It's always something really corny that starts it. Suddenly Julie's forgetting Cleopatra's name struck us all as the funniest thing since the rubber chicken.

We were laughing so hard by the time we got to the checkout that we could hardly talk. The salesgirl was leaning against the counter cracking her gum and looking totally bored. While she was sliding our stuff across the scanner her gum made a noise like a gunshot and Julie grabbed her chest, rolled her eyes back, and pretended she was hit. We all burst out laughing again. The salesgirl stopped what she was doing and looked at us like we were certifiable.

"I thought I heard a gun," Julie said with a straight face.

"Backfire," the girl said briefly.

This, of course, caused us to laugh harder.

"Backfires always crack us up," Julie said, by way of explanation.

"Sure," the girl said, and handed Julie the change. She flashed us an almost-grin. "Have a nice day."

That totally cracked us up and we laughed all the way to the food court. I was beginning to feel better than I had in days. The mood continued through our stop at the pizza place, where Allie, Becky, and I each had a slice of pizza and a medium soda. Julie had two slices of pizza, what was left of my slice, and a drink that was so large they called it "The Oasis."

The fabric store, Sew and Sew, is right next to the food court. We walked over there and picked out glue, beads, sequins, and some fabric to make appliqués with.

"Last stop, Cinderella," Becky said as we left the mall.

When we arrived at the boutique, Nicole was moving dresses from a floor rack to the racks on the sides of the store. Mom had told me that the center of the store would have to be cleared of everything but what she calls "the islands." There are three of them and to me they look sort of like those plastic swimming pools that little kids have. They are very light, although the sides look like real stone. You put them on the floor, and when they're filled with marble chips or bark chips they do look like little islands on the blue carpet of the store.

That season Mom had a huge palm plant on each of the islands along with a mannequin dressed in a linen shirt and shorts. Halfway toward the back of the store there are three steps going up to a second level, where there's some more clothing, the dressing room, and the door to the back room. On either side of the stairs were palm trees strung with wicker chains. There were bathing suits hung on the wicker chains along with cute wicker monkeys. That was my favorite display in the store. I should probably mention that I designed it.

"Hi," Nicole said. "Rosie, your mom is up by the dressing room with a customer."

"Hi, Nicole," we all responded. "I'm just going to pick up some stuff Mom's giving me," I added. "It's in the back room."

"Yeah, she told me about it," Nicole said. "Your party sounds great, Rosie. The fashion show is a really good idea."

"Allie thought of it first," I said.

"But Rosie has all the great ideas about fashion," Allie added. "That's how come we can't understand why—" Allie stopped abruptly and looked at me. "W-why . . ."

"Hi, honey," Mom called. "Are you here for the trim stuff?"

"Yeah, Mom."

"Let's look at the bathing suits," Julie said, pulling Allie and Becky toward a display.

I went to the upper level, where my mother was standing. A woman whom I recognized as a regular customer disappeared into the dressing room. Mom smiled at me and gave me a hug.

"Got your shopping done for the party?" she asked.

"Yeah, we're in good shape," I said.

"I wish I could say the same," Mom sighed. She looked tired.

"You know I'd help," I said.

"You have your party. But if . . ." She didn't finish because the customer called out for Mom to bring her the next size.

I left my mom to her customer and went to the back room, where I saw boxes of trims and buttons. Mom must have taken the time to sort out the stuff for me. I knew how busy she was, and it made me feel better that she had done that. At least she hadn't forgotten me completely.

When I came back to the front with the boxes, my friends were gathered around Nicole. She was showing them what Mom had planned for the fashion show.

"We're going to have a runway coming out from the top of the stairs and down to the middle of the store. We'll have chairs on either side. That's why I'm doing this." She waved her arms at the dresses she had moved. "We're redoing the windows, too. We want to have a lot of Lucienne stuff in the displays."

"Nice," Julie said.

Nicole turned to me. "Rosie, did your mom show you the list of clothes Lucienne is sending?" I shook my head. I wasn't really in the mood to talk to Nicole. Mom always says Nicole does a good job with the store's bookkeeping and with organizing the stock in the back room. But I knew I was a lot better at things like designing the window displays and dressing mannequins. And here was Nicole doing what I should have been doing! I didn't want to say anything that might sound bitter, so I just shook my head.

"Gee, I thought you'd have the list memorized by now," Nicole said.

"Well, I haven't had a chance to look at it yet," I said. It was not a lie. I hadn't had the chance to look at it because Mom hadn't shown it to me.

"They sound totally divine," Nicole said excitedly. Then she groaned. "But it sounds like a lot of work. Your mother wants me to organize everything according to—"

"Great, Nicole," I interrupted her. "We gotta go." Nobody seemed to be listening to me, though.

Nicole turned to Allie. "You should hear the names of the colors Lucienne is using this year. Aubergine—that means eggplant," she giggled.

"Yuck," Allie said.

"I love purple," Becky said.

"I love eggplant," Julie said.

I had to smile at Julie. It's probably a good thing that I did, since it kept me from blowing my top. The worst thing was, I didn't know who to blow up at. I knew it wasn't Nicole's fault that she was doing what I wanted to be doing. And I certainly couldn't be mad at Lucienne for coming to Canfield. But could I really be so mad at my own mother? I figured the best thing to do was get out of the store as quickly as possible.

"What else besides eggplant, Nicole?" Allie asked.

"Ah . . . something called saffron," Nicole said. "I'm not sure what color it is. There's a bunch of swatches someplace here. I laid them down just before you came in."

Julie and Becky started to look around. I didn't want to yell at them, but the more Nicole talked, the less patience I had. I wanted to leave before I ended up saying something nasty.

"Nicole," I said, pointing to the counter in the back, "I'm going to take a couple of shopping bags to put our stuff in. We've got a lot to carry."

"Sure, Rosie. Do you want me to get them for you?"

"I know where they are," I said.

I put all our packages together in two Cinderella shopping bags. Mom came out of the dressing room with a blond woman who was trying on a green silk sheath.

"Rosie, you know Ms. Payne, don't you?"

"There's a great paisley shawl up front," I pointed out. "It would look super with that dress."

"Really?" The woman turned and looked into the mirror. "Maybe I'll try it."

"Let me get it, Ms. Payne," Mom said. We walked down the stairs together and I took the shawl from the mannequin and handed it to my mom.

"You're right, Rosie," Mom said. "If this is draped right it will be very flattering on her." I was about to offer to help Ms. Payne arrange it properly, but Mom hurried back to the dressing room.

"I talked to Lucienne's secretary on the phone yesterday—" Nicole was saying as I came back to the front of the store.

"Interesting, Nicole," I said. "But we've really got to go."

"No problem." Nicole waved her hand and turned back to Becky and Julie. "The secretary was calling about hotel reservations for the models. They're going to get here next Saturday. I'll get to talk to them . . ."

I walked toward the door. I couldn't stand another minute of Nicole's chatter about the fashion show.

The fashion show that didn't include me.

Five

Saturday was a gorgeous day, too gorgeous to be feeling sad. I decided to put all my frustrations about Nicole and the fashion show behind me. I even jogged around the park before I started getting ready for Belinda's party.

Mom had gone into the store early so my dad gave me a ride to Belinda's house. We picked up Julie on the way.

The sunshine had obviously gotten to Julie, too. She started talking even before she got in the car. "Hi, Mr. Torres, thanks for picking me up. Rosie, can you come over to my house after the party? I need some help with my history homework."

"I guess so," I said, and looked at my dad. He nodded okay.

"Heather can give you a ride home," Julie

added. Then she went on, "I brought an old shirt of my dad's, like you told me. It's as if we're in kindergarten again! Remember when we had to wear a shirt backward while we were painting?"

"Decorating the T-shirts isn't going to be that messy, I hope," I said. "But you don't want to get the paint on anything good."

"These are my number one jeans," Julie said and laughed.

"You sure are in an up mood, today," I said.

"I took a bike ride this morning," Julie said happily.

I looked at her closely. She had a smile on her face that you don't get from an ordinary bike ride.

"Okay, spill, Berger," I said. "I can see you're dying to."

Julie giggled. "Mark Harris called me this morning and asked if I wanted to go on a bike ride. His brother's team was practicing at Van Fleet Park and Mark wanted to watch him pitch." Julie has a huge crush on Mark Harris, and from all the evidence, the feeling seems to be mutual.

My dad and Julie talked about baseball statistics for the rest of the ride. As we pulled up at the

Collinses' house, Becky's mom was just driving away.

"I'll take one of those bags," Julie said, hopping out. "Goodbye, Mr. Torres, and thanks again." She grabbed one of the shopping bags and ran up the drive.

"Julie must have eaten her Wheaties this morning," Dad observed wryly, waving to Julie.

I laughed. "Julie's usually like that."

As Julie and I walked into the house, Becky came in from the kitchen with a big basket on her arm. "Hi, guys," she said, putting the basket on the coffee table and picking up a delicate glass swan that had been sitting there. "Mrs. Collins is upstairs helping Belinda get dressed."

Julie and I were cautiously eyeing the glass swan in Becky's hand. Becky has many outstanding qualities. She's generous, creative, and a great friend, but she is also klutzy, In fact, if there were an Olympic medal for stumbling, Becky would get the gold without even trying.

"Hi." Allie came in from the dining room. "Want me to put that on the mantel, Becky?" Allie held her hand out.

"I'll put it on the bookcase, Allie." Becky

turned, caught her toe on the elaborate leg of the coffee table and started to pitch forward. Allie grabbed for her sweater at the same time as I reached for the swan, but after an elaborate flailing wiggle Becky saved herself. She pivoted around, holding the swan up in the air triumphantly. "I got it!" She grinned and we all let our breath out.

"If that thing got smashed," Allie said, "it would probably cost a lot more to replace than what we make on a party."

We all held our breath again as Becky stretched up on tiptoe to put the swan on the top shelf of the bookcase. She wobbled a bit, but the glass bird safely made it up to its new resting place.

"I've got the plastic forks and spoons rolled in napkins," Allie said. We followed her into the dining room. "I'm going to stack them on the sideboard buffet style, because I figure we'll be using the table for the T-shirt decorating."

"Good thinking," I said. "I'll get the table set up."

"First look at the cake, you two." Becky pointed to a small table placed in the corner of the room.

Matthew had made a huge sheet cake and had cut it into the shape of a T-shirt. He had glazed the whole thing with white frosting. Then he had gone to town, decorating the T-shirt with candy of all different shapes and colors. Across the front of the T-shirt was written Happy Birthday Belinda in bold magenta icing.

"I'm torn between wanting to eat this and wanting to wear it," Becky said.

"I say wear it," I said.

"I say eat it," Julie said.

Becky looked at Allie and they both started laughing. "Both of you keep your hands off," Becky said.

"Well, Matthew did a super job on the cake once again," I said.

We put all the candy in bowls and arranged them on the table.

"Have you got the pictures for the game?" I asked. Julie nodded.

I set all the decorating stuff in the middle of the table. There were bottles of fabric glue and paint, brushes, fabric markers, sequins, buttons, pieces of ribbon and lace, and a pile of little sponges cut in the shapes of animals.

"What are those sponges for?" Allie asked.

"Well, I was thinking about these shirts last night," I said. "You know, they could turn out to be disasters if we just let the kids go at them with the paint. So I made these with cookie cutters last night. I traced the outline on the sponge and cut it out with scissors." I picked up a sponge in the shape of a dog. "The kids can use them like a stamp. All they have to do is dip them in paint and press them on the shirt. After they've stamped designs on the shirts, they can glue or sew on other things, such as beads and sequins."

"That's a great idea, Rosie." Becky grabbed a sponge. "I love this bird one."

"Chalk another one up for Torres," Julie said.

"I did a T-shirt last night to show the kids what the paint looks like. I thought I'd give it to Belinda."

I unfolded the shirt. I had drawn a big sunburst with bright yellow paint, then used a black fabric marker to outline it. Finally I'd glued on sequins to make it sparkle.

"Rosie, it's awesome," Becky said.

Just then Mrs. Collins came into the dining room, Belinda tagging along shyly behind her.

Mrs. Collins raved about the sponge patterns and Belinda almost went into orbit when she saw the cake.

A few minutes later most of the guests had arrived. Becky and I set up the last of the T-shirt decorating materials while Julie and Allie got the first game started. After a girl named Annie had won (she was the first to guess correctly about the picture pinned to her back), we were finally ready to start the shirts. I showed them the shirt I had done and explained how to use the paint, glue, fabric markers, and sponges.

"Just dip it in the paint," I said holding up a sponge fish and pointing to the saucers of paint in the middle of the table. "Now you've probably all used a stamp pad, right?" The kids nodded. "Well, that's just how you use a sponge. Just stamp straight down on your shirt and quickly lift it up."

I stamped one several times on a napkin to show them. They couldn't wait to get started.

One little girl, Bethany, was so enthusiastic that she smeared her dog. She looked like she was going to cry, but Belinda grabbed the shirt and held it up, exclaiming, "Look, Bethany's dog looks like he's running."

The kids all laughed and Bethany beamed. "I'm going to stamp a picture of a kitten on the other side for the dog to be chasing." She proceeded to do just that, then glued buttons on the animals for eyes and put bows made of gold cord around their necks. It really looked cute.

When the shirts were all done we laid them out to dry. While we were waiting, we served cake and ice cream, and then Belinda unwrapped her gifts. She absolutely loved the T-shirt I had decorated.

After a quick check of the shirts, Becky announced, "Come on, everybody, your shirts are ready to put on for the fashion show."

When they had all donned their creations, they lined up and I did a little makeover on each of them. I kept the makeup to a minimum. When they had finished admiring each other Allie and Becky took the kids out into the hall.

"I'll get the camera," I said.

"Give me a yell when you're ready," Julie said. "I'll get the music ready."

"Girls," Mrs. Collins said, coming to the door, "some of the parents are here. Can we all come in and watch?"

"Sure," Julie said. "The kids will probably love an audience."

The parents came in and sat in the living room. Then Becky stuck her head around the corner. "Music!" she called. Julie started the tape and the kids marched out into the living room.

Belinda's mother and the other parents joined Becky and Allie in clapping for every kid while I snapped pictures of them. We planned to take the film to a one-hour developing place and send them to the kids as party favors.

From the kids' laughter and the parents' comments after the fashion parade, the party seemed to be a real success. Allie had placed a stack of Party Line flyers on a table by the door. All the parents took one on the way out.

When we had cleaned up and were scarfing down the last of the birthday cake and sodas, Julie held up her soda can. "I want to make a toast," she said. "To us. Another smashing party."

Becky giggled. "Even better," she said. "We had a smashing party without smashing anything."

Six

My family has a rule that nothing disagreeable can be discussed at the dinner table. I came very close to reminding my mom of that rule Tuesday night.

It seemed that preparations for the fashion show hadn't been going as smoothly as she had thought they would. We had just sat down at the table when Mom started telling us about all the problems at Cinderella. "I'm run ragged trying to coordinate this show and run the store, too." She was spooning broccoli onto her plate. "I don't mind the work, of course, but—"

Dad and I were both staring at her plate. "Whoa," Dad interrupted her. "You must be hungry." He pointed to the mountain of broccoli on her plate.

Mom laughed and started spooning it back into the serving dish. "That's a perfect example of what I've been doing at the store all day."

"I take it things are getting a little hectic," my dad said.

"Hectic is the nicest way to put it," she said. "The worst part is that it's my own fault. Lucienne told me that she didn't want things to be too hard on us and suggested we should keep it simple. But I want the show in Canfield to be the best in the whole tour, so I just waded in—and now I'm in up to my eyeballs."

"I understand wanting to do your best," Dad said.

Mom shrugged. "In this case, I decided my best was an elevated runway to show the clothes to their best advantage."

Dad and I nodded. We had heard about that.

"Well, I borrowed platforms from the school." Mom turned to me. "They're the ones you helped make for *Romeo and Juliet*." The seventh and eighth grades had recently done a production of Shakespeare's play. Becky was the star and I worked on sets.

"Great, Mom," I said without enthusiasm. At

least I could say I had contributed *something* to the fashion show.

"So I called Lucienne today and told her about the runway. She said she never expected professional staging, but she was thrilled to have it," my mom said.

"It must be nice to hear that she appreciates what you've done," Dad said.

Mom nodded. "Lucienne also said that she would love to have me do the show commentary with her," Mom went on. "She said I seem to be so proficient and professional that she knows I would do a superb job."

"Mom, that's fantastic!" I gasped.

Mom nodded gloomily. "But now I have to find two microphones and two podiums!"

Dad laughed. "You make it sound like a punishment."

Mom sighed. "I think I've really overextended myself this time."

"Are you nervous, Mom?" I asked.

"A bit, honey. I did some public speaking in college, but this is more than I bargained for. I thought I would just stand there with Lucienne and smile while she introduced the models and described the fashions. I didn't realize she wanted me to take over the narration from time to time."

"I'll tell you what," I piped up. "I'll do it for you. Okay?"

Mom smiled, but I could tell it was just one of those absent smiles that meant she hadn't really heard what I had said.

"If it's too much, just decline the offer," Dad said.

"But Lucienne is doing it as a favor to me," Mom said. "She told me she had never worked with anyone who was so enthusiastic and she wants me to be right by her side so that I get the recognition I deserve."

"Hooray for Lucienne," I said. "You know a lot of the top designers would never share the spotlight with anyone."

"Rosie's right," Dad said.

"I have to memorize the whole lineup," Mom continued. "And that's in addition to a million other things. Like the chairs."

"I thought you were renting them," I said.

"I did," she replied. "And they came today."

"Today?" Both Dad and I spoke at the same time.

"Not only was it the wrong day, they were the wrong chairs," Mom said, "and the worst of all, they were old metal folding chairs that had the words Meyers Funeral Home stenciled on the back."

Both Dad and I burst out laughing, but when we caught the look on Mom's face we stopped.

"I took care of it," she said wearily. "The rental people were all apologies. They told me that those chairs were old ones that they never rent out; they only lend them to nonprofit organizations for free. It seems that the public library is putting on a children's production of Cinderella this weekend," Mom explained, "and I guess they got their Cinderellas mixed up."

"It sounds like you have everything under control," Dad said, "but if you need any help let me know."

"Thanks, sweetheart, but I already planned to ask Rosie," Mom said.

Suddenly the pie I was eating tasted heavenly. She was going to ask me to work on the show!

"Mom, you know I'll do anything." I tried to keep my voice down to a medium shriek. "I've dreamed about helping Lucienne . . ."

"Now wait, Rosie." Mom held up her hand. I guess she wanted to stop me before I started doing cartwheels in the dining room. "What I really need is for you to help put those platforms together for the runway."

My bubble didn't burst completely, but it was severely deflated. "I'll come over right after school," I said, trying not to let my disappointment show. Putting platforms together. It wasn't exactly the job of a burgeoning fashion star, but at least I had gotten my foot in the door.

The next day at lunch Becky asked us all to come over after school to visit Gemini. I told her I couldn't go and I explained to them about the problems that my mom was having.

"You know, Rosie," Becky said, "you can count on us for help if you need it." Allie and Julie agreed.

I smiled. "Thanks, you guys. I'll let you know."

During the ride home on the bus I tried to recall every detail that I had learned when I helped on the stage crew of *Romeo and Juliet*. I figured a fashion show would be a lot like any staged production. Ms. Marlow, the teacher who had directed *Romeo and Juliet,* had taught us how to do almost everything totally professionally.

I would do the same for this show, I decided. I hoped what they say in the theater is true—that there is no such thing as a small part, only small actors. I promised myself that I would do my very best, no matter how small and unimportant my job seemed.

When I arrived at Cinderella, I could see that things were not business as usual. First of all, the double doors were open; there were stacks of boards lying in front of them, and more piled on the sidewalk. Mom was standing just inside the doors talking to Fred, the man who does the lifting and hauling for her when she changes the store around. He also takes the trash from the back room once a week. He's the handyman for most of the small stores on Cinderella's block. Fred is really old. At least I think he is. He always tells me he knew my mom when she was knee-high to a grasshopper.

Fred had his hat off and was staring intently at the pile of boards when I came into the store. When he saw me he laughed and said, "Well, if it isn't my friend Rosie!" Fred has a big, booming voice that used to scare me when I was little.

"Hi, Fred. How's it going?"

"Slow, mighty slow."

Fred says that every time I ask him how things are going. So things were normal with *him*, at least. I stepped over a load of lumber.

"Rosie, I'm so glad you're here," my mom said. "Do you see this mess?"

I don't think she wanted an answer to that question because no one, not even someone a mile away, could miss the lumber piled on the sidewalk.

"I didn't realize the platform would arrive in so many pieces," Mom said. "I don't know what we're going to do with this mess."

"I do," I said. "First we should move everything into the store. Those big pieces there are the risers. They're just sheets of plywood. You attach different-length legs to each piece according to the height you want it."

Mom sighed. "That's the first thing that's made sense this afternoon. Rosie, you're a lifesaver."

"We did a play at school and I helped build the set," I explained to Fred. "That's how I know about legs and risers and things. I'll get my jeans on and we can get started." I headed for the dressing room in the back.

When I came out, Fred had all the two-by-fours sorted by length and had emptied the bag of C-clamps and six-inch bolts on the floor. He was looking at it all a little doubtfully.

"I'm not sure these are going to hold up," he said.

"You'd be surprised how strong each riser is once the legs are clamped on. You use six legs on every one," I said. "We had kids dancing on them in the play."

Fred picked up a leg with a number three marked on it and, before I could explain, started to clamp it on the riser that was also marked number three. "It's like putting a puzzle together," he said.

We worked together the rest of the afternoon. Fred wanted me to tell him all the stage-carpentry jargon I had learned. It didn't take him long to catch on.

I helped Fred calculate exactly how many risers we'd need to bring the runway from the top of the steps down to the front of the store and what height legs were required.

"As I see it," Fred said, "we're going to need twenty-four-inch legs to bring the front risers up to the right level." I agreed and sorted through the pile for the twenty-four-inchers.

As she watched us put the runway together, Mom smiled for the first time that afternoon. "You two are doing a great job," she said. "I'll go back and see how Nicole is doing with the boxes that came today."

I jumped up. "Did Lucienne's clothes come today?" A few legs clattered to the floor.

"Only the accessories, hon," my mom said. "I have Nicole unpacking them now. You'll help more if you stay here with Fred and get this job done. You can look over the accessories anytime."

"Oh. Sure. Well, don't give the runway another thought, Mom. Fred and I have it under control," I told her. Disappointment was getting to be a pretty familiar feeling with this fashion show.

When we finished getting the runway put together, I pulled several huge pieces of black material from the canvas bag.

"It's the skirt," I said. "It hides the legs and clamps."

When the skirt was on, Fred and I stood back and admired our work. He looked over at me and his eyes were twinkling. "You'll do," he said. Mom had told me that was Fred's highest compliment, and so I beamed. As he was putting his tools away he offered to help when Canfield Middle School did its next production.

"Thanks, Fred," I said.

"I'll clean up here, Rosie," he said. "You go and take a load off the floor."

That was Fred's way of saying that I should sit down and relax. I immediately headed back to see what accessories Lucienne had sent.

Nicole was taking tags off scarfs and putting them on hangers. There was a row of shoeboxes and a shelf heaped with piles of earrings, pins, and bracelets.

I picked up a pin that was almost as big as a saucer. It was a stylized sunburst made out of lightweight wood and painted in brilliant oranges and yellows. It reminded me of the sun I had painted on the T-shirt at Belinda's party. *I guess*

Lucienne and I think alike about some things, I said to myself. The thought made me smile.

"Spectacular, isn't it?" Mom had come up in back of me. She kissed the top of my head.

"Yeah." I nodded.

"Nicole," Mom said, "you've been cooped up back here for hours. Why don't you take a break? Go outside and take a little walk in the sunshine."

"Thanks a lot, Mrs. Torres. I'll go to the deli and get us some iced tea."

"She's been working really hard," Mom said as Nicole left the back room. I had a twinge of guilt at the mean things I had said about her.

"And you did a wonderful job up front. Fred said that he thinks you're Wonder Woman in training." Mom laughed. "I told him you were Wonder Woman already."

"Gee, thanks, Mom," I said. "Does that mean I can ask for a raise in my allowance?"

Mom laughed, then she sat down and put her feet up. She patted the chair beside her and I sat down, too. "I can't tell you how much I appreciate all your help, honey," she said. "I sometimes forget that I should tell you that, instead of assuming you know how important you are. But I

have been running around here like a chicken
with its head cut off and I've forgotten a lot of
things."

"I understand," I said.

"I realize it has been thoughtless of me to wait
so long to ask you this," Mom went on, "but will
you join the crew for the show on Sunday?"

It didn't sink in at first. I sat quietly, still trying
to think up good arguments why my mother
should let me help with the show. Then it finally
hit me.

"Does that mean working back here instead of
watching the show from the audience?" I finally
squeaked.

"Yes, I would like you to work back here with
Nicole and the mod—"

"Back here?" I yelped.

"Uh-huh."

"Helping *Lucienne?*"

She nodded. "It's a small job but—"

"It's enormous!" I blurted. "Don't you know
there are no small jobs?" I was practically doing a
jig around the room.

Nicole returned to the back room with a card-
board holder full of cold drinks.

"I'm going to work back here with you, Nicole!" I cried. Suddenly Nicole seemed like the most wonderful person on earth.

"Great. Maybe you can help me figure out how to arrange all these accessories."

"No problem," I said gleefully.

Later I remembered something that my dad once told me: When somebody says "no problem," there's definitely a problem.

Seven

Thursday was one of those days when school seems to drag on forever. That's always the way it is when you're waiting for something.

The clothes for the fashion show were supposed to have been delivered Wednesday afternoon, but they hadn't come. So I raced to the store as soon as school got out that afternoon to see if anything had been delivered. Nothing. At six o'clock my mom sent Nicole home. By eight o'clock we had given up on the delivery and were about to turn off the lights and go home when someone banged on the front door. Lo and behold, the truck had arrived. Two hours later, after a whole lot of heavy labor, Lucienne's stock was safe in our back room.

The trunks that Lucienne had sent were made

of canvas stretched over a frame of thin metal bars. They looked heavy, but they moved as easily as skateboards because they were on wheels. Their wooden tops were padlocked shut.

When the truck was gone, Mom and I stood looking at the ten huge trunks. "Rosie, I think I've bitten off more than I can chew," my mom said. "How will we ever get all these trunks unpacked?"

"I have an idea, Mom," I said. "I'll call Allie, Becky and Julie when we get home. I know they'd be glad to help. I think all this unpacking would cost you roughly two pizzas with mushrooms and pepperoni and a side order of fries for Julie."

Mom laughed. "It's a deal. I'll even throw in brownie sundaes."

Even though it was after ten, I called Julie as soon as I got home to tell her about the unpacking job. She volunteered her help immediately and said she would start the phone chain right away. She would have Becky call me to tell me whether she and Allie could help also.

Mom and I were having sandwiches and milk when Becky called a few minutes later to tell me that both she and Allie were ready and willing as well. I told her that my mom would pick us up after school the next day.

I hung up and went back to my sandwich, smiling to myself. I was exhausted but totally blissed out. Not only was I going to work on the fashion show, but I had the greatest friends in the whole world!

Julie plopped down against the wall by the school's side door. "I can't wait to see the rags," she said.

"Rags!" Allie gasped. "These aren't rags, Julie! These are original Luciennes."

Julie, Becky, and I laughed. Allie's a great person, but she's so serious-minded that she almost never gets jokes.

"Relax, Allie," Julie said. "Heather says that's what they call clothes in the New York fashion business. She should know—she reads every fashion magazine published."

"I don't care what they do in New York. I'd never call Lucienne's things rags," Becky said.

"Not at what they cost," Allie added.

"I think I see your mom's car," Julie said.

"Let's meet her at the end of the driveway," I

said. "She'll never get through the mob." It was such a gorgeous day that a lot of kids were hanging out in front of school.

We had just started down the drive when someone called, "Hey, Torres, wait up."

Of all people, it was Casey Wyatt. He was on his bike and he was headed right for me.

"Wow, Rosie," Julie said. "I think Casey likes you."

"The last time Casey called my name it was so he could aim a spitball directly at my eye," I said.

Julie laughed. "Aw, he's just shy—that's his way of telling you he cares."

Casey swerved his bike between my friends and me.

"What do you want, Casey? I've got to go. My mom's here."

"We'll tell your mom you'll be a few minutes," Becky giggled as she, Julie, and Allie ran down the drive.

"Where do you get tickets for that fashion show at your mother's store?" He was almost whispering.

"The fashion show?"

"Yeah, yeah. You don't have to advertise it all over."

I almost laughed in his face. Maybe there was a side to Casey that I didn't know about. "You want some fashion tips?"

"It's not for me, you dork." Casey whipped his head around to see who was within hearing distance. He was definitely the same old Casey.

"Then why do you want tickets?" I asked.

Casey looked around again. "It's my mother's birthday and I thought she'd like it."

I knew Casey's mother. She was a really nice person, even if she was partly responsible for the most obnoxious boy in the seventh grade. I'm sure it was worse for her than it was for me—after all, she had to put up with Casey all the time at home!

"You can buy them at Cinderella," I said.

"How much?" His face looked a little red. Was Casey Wyatt blushing?

"Fifteen dollars each," I said. "But they're almost gone, so you'd better—"

I didn't have time to finish because he took off so fast his tires kicked up gravel against my legs.

When I got to the car Becky, Allie, and Julie

had already piled into the back seat. "Great friends you guys are," I said as I got into the front seat.

"We didn't want to get in your way in case Casey was asking you out," Becky said, and they all roared with laughter.

"They can be *so* childish at times," I said loftily to Mom, but she was laughing right along with them.

"So what did he want?" Julie asked.

"Tickets to the fashion show," I said.

That shut them up.

"You've got to be kidding!" Becky said.

"Maybe he's going to be a designer," Julie hooted.

"His rags really would be rags," Allie said.

"If it's a Wyatt, don't buy it," Becky quipped. We all cracked up.

We were still laughing about Casey when we drove up to Cinderella.

"Look," Allie yelled, "there's Casey! He's already leaving."

"He must have flown down here," Mom said.

"The boy has a lot of energy, Mrs. Torres," Julie said.

"Then maybe I should ask him to help unpack," Mom said.

There was a chorus of groans from the back seat. "No, please!" Julie said. "No Casey."

"We'll do all the work," Becky said. "Just don't ask Casey."

Mom smiled, "Okay, okay. I'll let you out in front. I have to run to the florist to check on the flowers for the show."

When we went into the back room we saw Fred fumbling with a pile of aluminum pipes that looked like a modern-art piece. Nicole was dragging garment bags out of one of the trunks. "These are really awkward," she said. "They're so bulky."

"Where shall we start?" Becky asked.

"I'll help with those metal things." Julie grinned at Fred.

"I wouldn't say no to some help," Fred said gratefully.

I was dying to get to the clothes, but I asked Nicole where I could be the most help. After all, she was Mom's assistant, and I was supposed to take orders from her when my mother wasn't there. Plus I wanted this to be the best fashion show ever and I wasn't about to let my puny ego get in the way.

"Thanks, Rosie." Nicole smiled at me. "Would you mind hanging up the clothes as soon as Fred and Julie get the racks put together? Your mother left instructions to get them on hangers as soon as possible so the wrinkles will fall out."

Julie laughed. "It's a dirty job, Nicole, but Rosie knows someone has to do it."

Nicole smiled. "I have to figure out how Lucienne wants them hung. There are two pages of notes explaining her system, but I can't read half of them, and I can't understand the other half."

"Nicole, maybe we should figure out the notes before we start taking the stuff out of the trunks," I said.

"Yes," Allie agreed. "If there are two pages of notes, she must want things done in a very particular way. Would you like me to take a look at them?"

"Would you? I was worried I'd have to send them to the FBI to have them decoded." Nicole handed two dog-eared sheets of paper to Allie.

By the time my mom got back to the store, we were all hanging up clothes. Fred and Julie had gotten all the racks put together and arranged in a row. And after Allie had deciphered Lucienne's handwriting she had no trouble figuring out how the designer wanted the clothes arranged.

"Mrs. Torres, this is a super system." Allie was grinning from ear to ear. We don't call her Organized Allie for nothing.

"Allie, I've been so pressed for time, I haven't had a chance to read Lucienne's notes. Would you explain them to me?"

That was all Allie needed to hear. Next thing we knew, she was off and running. "The clothes are all marked with a colored dot on the inside, and each is supposed to be hung on a hanger of the same color." Allie pointed to a full rack. "Each of the models has a color assigned to her, so that all she has to do is glance at a rack to know what she'll be wearing."

Mom nodded and went over to one of the racks. "I see. The racks are numbered, too," she said.

Allie motioned to the number one on the front of that rack. "Exactly. They are numbered one through eight, like the hangers. So there is a red hanger numbered one, two, three, and so on. The show starts with rack one."

"How clever," Mom said.

"Isn't it?" Allie agreed. "And the hangers are arranged in a certain color order on each rack: red, orange, yellow, green, blue, and purple."

"Lucienne certainly is organized," Mom said.

"I know." Allie sighed blissfully.

I sighed with ecstasy at exactly the same time. I had just taken a plastic garment bag off the most beautiful thing I had ever seen. It was a short patchwork blazer with long, tapered sleeves. The colors in the patchwork pattern were deep jewel tones of ruby, emerald, sapphire, and topaz. It was pure silk and as soft as a whisper.

For the rest of the afternoon at the store and even at the pizza parlor where Mom treated us all for supper afterward, I couldn't get the vision of the jacket out of my mind. I kept seeing it in different combinations, ranging from casual to formal wear. Of course in my daydream I was the one wearing it, even though I knew I would never really be able to wear it. It would probably take ten years of allowance to buy it. But I enjoyed an elaborate fantasy of walking down the runway in a silk gown with the jacket casually thrown over my shoulder. I could dream, couldn't I?

Eight

Saturday morning at our house was prime chaos. Lucienne had called to say that she and her models had just arrived, and Mom was going to meet them at Cinderella in forty-five minutes. Meanwhile Mom was sitting at the table staring at her notebook as if she were cramming for an exam. Dad offered to make the coffee, but he spilled the whole can on the floor. I cleaned it up while he heated water for instant coffee. Then he burned the first two bagels he toasted. I took over at the toaster, and Dad put a cup of watery coffee in front of Mom with an apologetic grin. My Dad is actually perfectly competent in the kitchen. I think he was nervous for my mom. He was trying so hard to help, he was just making everything worse.

She mumbled her thanks and proceeded to stir her coffee with her pencil. Dad and I broke up.

"What are you two laughing at?" Mom said.

"Your charming and original method of stirring coffee," Dad said.

"Thank you." Mom smiled and went back to her notes.

Mom finished her coffee, looked up at the clock, and put her mug down with a bang. "I have to leave for the store right away. Lucienne and the models are probably already there. Rosie, do you want to come with me now, or do you want Dad to bring you over later?" She was already on her way out of the kitchen.

"Better go with her, honey," Dad said. "Don't let her read her notebook while she's driving," he said in a stage whisper. Mom playfully tossed a potholder at him and went into the garage.

I grabbed half a bagel and quickly smeared cream cheese on it. "I know how she feels, Dad. I'm nervous, too." Actually, I think I was even more excited than Mom. After all, she had been talking with Lucienne on the phone for weeks, but this would be my first chance to say anything to her. I wanted to make a good impression. I had given myself a facial the night before and had spent hours picking out the perfect outfit.

Mom had already started the car when I ran out of the house. She handed me her notebook. "Rosie, would you read this list to me while I drive?"

"Okay, Mom." I couldn't hold both my bagel and the notebook, so I carefully laid my bagel on the dashboard.

"Okay. What's the first thing on that page?" Mom asked.

"Food," I said.

"Right. I'm so glad you reminded me that the Moondance caters parties."

"I'm glad I did, too," I said. "Even though Becky said her mother has been keeping her busy polishing all their silver serving-trays and candle-sticks."

"Marilyn showed me the silver when I went there to talk with her and Russell about what to serve. Some of it has been in her family for years," Mom said. "The refreshment table is going to be really elegant."

"Great, Mom. I know the food will be—"

Suddenly Mom stomped on the brakes and the

car shuddered to a stop. The bagel slid off the dashboard onto my jeans—cream cheese side down.

"I don't believe it. I almost ran that red light," Mom said. "What were you saying, Rosie?"

"Cheese, Mom. I love it every place but on my best jeans."

"What? Oh, dear."

I picked up the gooey thing and held it out toward her. "Want a bite?"

"Don't get me laughing, honey. I've got to keep sane this morning."

The store seemed to be in good shape when we arrived. I hoped that Lucienne would think so, too. The clothes were all hung on their racks according to color and number. Nicole had rearranged all the accessories she'd unpacked on Wednesday and put them in boxes, where they would be right at our fingertips the next day.

I was in the dressing room trying to scrub the cream cheese spot off my jeans when Mom yelled, "They're here."

Wouldn't you know it? The most glamorous designer in the world comes to my mother's shop and I'm wearing my breakfast on my pants. I sighed. I was sure Lucienne would think I was some kind of spaz who couldn't navigate a bagel to her mouth. I smoothed my hair back and tightened the clip. Too tight. I pulled the barrette out and glanced in the mirror. My hair looked like I'd been caught in a hurricane. I took a deep breath and addressed myself in the mirror.

"Rosie Torres," I said, "you are being silly. Fix your hair, and put on some lip gloss and get out there and meet Lucienne."

I could have picked out Lucienne in a crowd of a million people. But it was a lot easier than that. There were six tall girls standing in the middle of the store holding small suitcases. They had scarves around their hair and were wearing sunglasses. There was one short lady in a black dress with an old-fashioned knitting bag on her arm. Then there was Lucienne. She was tall and gorgeous. Her blond hair was short and spiky. She had on a simple two-piece dress in bright orange and a zillion gold chains around her neck. She was looking around the store and from the smile on her face I guessed that she liked what she saw.

She started introducing the models to Mom as they all moved back toward the dressing room.

Cinderella had only one dressing room. Fortunately it was huge. The walls were papered in a floral print called "English Garden," and there was an antique chaise and a couple of comfortable chairs. Mom had scattered several beautiful screens around so customers could have as much privacy as they wanted. There were two old brass clothes poles, and the walls were hung with antique mirrors. There was a bathroom right off the dressing room and also a door leading into the back room.

Mom and Fred had set up a long table lined with mirrors for makeup and hair. Fred had installed electrical outlets for curling irons and hair dryers. Mom had also supplied the dressing room with a cooler full of ice and mineral water and a large basket of fruit. The basket looked great on the wicker table. I felt really proud of my mom as I glanced around the dressing room.

Mom put her arm around my shoulders. "Lucienne, I'd like you to meet my daughter, Rosie. She's been a huge help with the show."

Lucienne smiled at me. I could actually feel my legs turning to butter.

The designer held out her hand. "Hello, Rosie. Thank you for helping. I appreciate it."

I shook it and mumbled something really clever, like "Uh, hi, uh, I was glad . . . uh . . ."

Mom laughed. "I've never seen Rosie at a loss for words before. I know she couldn't wait to meet you."

I nodded vigorously. I was beginning to feel like a mime or something. I was just about to tell her that she was my very favorite designer when she pointed at my black sweatshirt.

It was one that I had decorated myself with the leftover paint from our fashion party. I had used gold fabric paint to draw big chains on the front of the shirt. Then I had glued on big fake jewels and even painted a watch hanging from one of the chains. It was sort of a copy of a Lucienne sweater from the previous year's collection.

Lucienne winked at me. "They say imitation is the sincerest form of flattery."

I could feel my face get hot, and my tongue was busy tying itself into a knot. I could only stammer, "Er . . . uh, yeah."

"These are my models." Lucienne waved at the six girls. "Tanya, the twins, Mindy and Meg,

Zivia, Gabby, and Kiki. And this is Babette, who keeps us all together." Lucienne put her arm around the short woman in the black dress.

"With needle and thread," Babette added. "The way those clothes are mistreated, I don't get a moment's rest." She gave the models a look that plainly said she thought *they* were the ones who mistreated the clothes. The girls must have been used to her, because they didn't seem to mind.

Lucienne hugged the older woman. "It's true, we couldn't survive without you."

"I only hope you have a good sewing machine for me," Babette said.

"We do," Mom said. "The fabric store lent it to me. It does everything. Let me show you." Mom motioned to the back room. "I had Fred put the machine out there with the clothes racks. Would you rather have it in the dressing room? I can have him move it."

"Definitely not in the dressing room with them," Babette snorted. She followed Mom to the back room.

"She's a little ornery," Meg said to me.

"But she's a miracle worker with her needle," Mindy said. The rest of them nodded.

Lucienne turned to me. "The dressing room is charming, Rosie." She sighed. "Well, I'd better go save your mother from Babette. Could you help install the girls?"

"Sure," I said. Lucienne hurried after Mom.

"This is a great store, Rosie," Tanya said. She pulled off her scarf. She had curling rods in her hair.

"The runway is just like the ones they have in big fashion houses," Gabby said.

Gabby wanted to know about food as soon as she put her suitcase down. I explained that Mom had made arrangements with a deli down the street to send someone over to take orders for lunch.

"You'll love the food from the deli," I told her. "I've known the Generellis for ages. They're really nice people, and their deli is the best!"

"Generelli." Gabby licked her lips. "I'm getting visions of pasta."

"They do have great pasta," I said. I was thinking that I'd have to tell Julie that this tall, gorgeous model seemed to think about food almost as much as she does.

"Never fear," Julie yelled, "The Party Line is here."

I ran out of the dressing room just in time to see Julie, Allie, and Becky stopped in their tracks halfway up the stairs, staring at Babette. "What's all this racket?" Babette said.

"These are my friends," I said. "They helped get things organized."

Fred came up behind Babette. "Well, the gang's all here," he said. "Couldn't have this show without 'em."

"Hi, Fred," Julie said. "Did the racks hold up?"

"Like the pyramids." Fred winked at us, then led Babette into the back room.

"Is she a good witch or a bad witch?" Julie whispered.

I giggled. "She's the seamstress," I said. "I guess we'd better keep out of her way."

"We just stopped in on our way over to my house to see Gemini," Becky said. "We wanted to get a peek at Lucienne and the models," she added in a low voice.

"Lucienne is in the back room. And the models are in the dressing room. You should see them. One is more beautiful than the next."

"I'd love to meet them," Allie said.

Just then the dressing-room door opened and Mindy came out. "Have you seen Babette?"

"She went into the back room," I said.

"With Fred," Julie hissed into my ear.

Mindy smiled at Allie, who was gazing up at her. "Hi," the model said.

"Hi," Allie said.

"Mindy, this is my friend Allie Gray," I said.

The rest of the models came to the door and smiled as I introduced my friends.

"Allie's the one who broke the code of Lucienne's notes," I explained.

All the models started laughing. They knew exactly what I was talking about.

"Uh . . . h-h." Allie stutters a little when she gets nervous. She waved her hand and managed a nervous "Hi."

"You liked the color system?" Zivia asked her. "It's my own creation."

"I think it's brilliant," Allie said.

"A girl after my own heart."

My friends gaped at the models for a few more minutes before they left Cinderella with a promise to come back in a few hours. Nicole arrived a little while later and my mom called her into the office to explain how they were going to handle the orders the next day.

I would have loved to talk to Lucienne about my interest in designing, but I could see that it wasn't going to happen. She was like a tornado. She had Fred move the podiums and microphones about a dozen times before she was satisfied.

Nicole didn't mind taking orders from Lucienne. She followed the designer around with a notebook, jotting down everything Lucienne said before passing it all on to me.

"Rosie, can you get some French-roast coffee? It's Lucienne's favorite."

"Okay, I'll ask Jimmy Generelli if they have it," I said.

"Oh, and there are boxes of special lemon-scented wipes that came in one of the trunks. Lucienne asked that whoever helps the models dress please wipe their hands on them between changes so the clothes don't get soiled. I put them on a shelf in the back room. Can you find them and get them out for tomorrow?"

"Sure, Nicole."

"And your mom wants to know if you would run

to the drugstore and get a can of anti-static spray."

As much as I wanted a chance to talk to Lucienne, I spent my morning being a gofer. When I got back from the errands, Jimmy Generelli was just leaving. "Hi, Rosie. Boy, have you ever seen so many beautiful women in one place?" He went out the door just as the rental company's truck drove up with the chairs—the right ones this time. They were little gold-colored chairs with mauve velvet seats. I opened the double doors so the delivery men could bring the chairs in. I spent the next half-hour setting them up.

Jimmy came back loaded down with boxes and bags. After the models had eaten and set up their makeup cases and hair dryers, they decided to take a look at Canfield. Mom gave them directions to the Canfield Inn, where she had booked rooms. She had to take Lucienne to the local TV station, where the designer was going to tape an interview that would be aired the next day on the evening news.

When they left, Nicole sat in one of the chairs and let out a long sigh. "I'd better sit now, because I don't think I'll get another chance the whole weekend."

I just nodded absent-mindedly at her. I was thinking that I hadn't even had a chance to talk to Lucienne after our introduction that morning.

Just then Fred came out of the back room to tell us that the flowers had arrived. Nicole and I hurried out to the back alley, where a florist's truck was unloading. Mom had ordered low white potted plants to go all around the runway to mask the wires and the footlights. We had just gotten all the plants into the shop when Julie, Allie, and Becky came back.

"Just in time to help with the plants," Fred greeted them.

They were glad to pitch in. Even Babette lent a hand in arranging the plants around the runway. When it was finished Fred switched the lights on and everyone sighed. It looked beautiful.

"Quitting time," I said.

"Rosie, we've come to take you out to dinner," Julie said.

"You guys are great," I said. I called Dad and asked him if it was okay. He agreed.

"We're out of here," I said.

As we walked down the street we tried to decide between the pizza parlor or the Burger Barn. I was too tired to care what we ate, so I let Julie talk us into the Burger Barn.

"Hey, Rosie, what's up? You're pretty quiet," Julie said as we all walked down Main Street.

"Nothing much. It's just that I was so excited to meet Lucienne this morning. I had gone over in my mind a thousand times what I would say to her, but when the time came I acted like an idiot. The worst part was, I never got another chance to talk to her," I said.

Just then we passed Le Bon Repas, a very expensive French restaurant. I glanced toward the entrance, then started to grin.

"What is it?" Allie said, noticing.

I pointed. Just going into the restaurant were Fred and Babette—arm in arm!

Nine

Sunday afternoon, Mom was in the back room of the store clutching her pearls. They were real pearls that had been in Dad's family for a hundred years. I knew she must be nervous because she had a death grip on them. "I'm just waiting for something to go wrong," she said.

"Like your pearls to go rolling down the runway," I giggled.

She gave me a little smile. "Don't try to make me feel better. I think if I feel awful now, then I won't feel awful later."

Sometimes I can't figure grownups out. "Mom, we've worked hard to make sure nothing can go wrong."

"Listen to your daughter, darling." Lucienne came up behind us. She had a long-stemmed yellow rose in her hand. She held it out to me.

I knew it was her trademark. I knew almost everything I could about her. In fact my own red rose trademark was similar to hers.

"Thank you," I said.

Lucienne turned to Mom. "Everything is perfect. The seats are all filled. The girls are ready. Now what could go wrong?"

"Well, I just have this feeling," Mom said.

Lucienne took my mom's arm. "Come on, we'll go out front. Stop worrying, nothing is going to go wrong."

The twins, Meg and Mindy, came out and looked over the clothes racks. When they stood together they looked like mirror images. Their makeup was perfect: deep red lipstick with blush and eye shadow in several tones of brown.

Kiki came into the back room in a silk wrapper. Her hair had hot rollers still wound on the crown. I must have had a surprised look on my face because she smiled and said, "It only takes me a second to get these out." She sniffed the air for a second, then smiled at Gabby, who was leaning over the sink splashing water on her face. "Mmm . . . I smell guacamole."

Gabby reached for a towel and came to the door

patting her face. "It's my recipe for dry skin: olive oil, honey, and avocado."

If I could have Gabby's exquisite skin, I thought, *I'd not only rub her recipe on my face, I'd drench my salad with it and drink it before bed.* I was putting white sheets on the floor for the models to stand on while they were changing outfits. Suddenly Nicole was at my elbow, looking very pale. "Rosie," she hissed. "Where is your mother?"

I could tell by the look on Nicole's face that something was wrong.

"What's the matter, Nicole?"

"Rosie, you know the color system that Lucienne uses?"

"Uh-huh."

She grabbed my arm. "The accessories, the jewelry and belts and scarves, that came the other day . . ."

"Yeah, what about them?" I tried to pry her hand from my arm.

"Well, they were all packed in plastic bags with little colored dots on them." Nicole let go of my arm and clenched her fists at her waist.

"Yeah, it makes it very simple."

"Well, I didn't know about the system then."
Nicole's voice had risen to a squeak. "I took all the
stuff out of the plastic bags. I arranged the stuff
the way I thought it should be. You know, belts
with belts and all the jewelry together." Nicole
was close to tears. "I didn't realize that I was
supposed to arrange them according to those
dumb colored dots. Now I have no idea what
accessories go with what outfit."

I just stared at her, stunned.

"What will I do, Rosie? Tanya is the first model
to go out and she needs me to accessorize her."

I wanted to yell for Mom, but I could already
hear music from the front of the store. That
meant that the fashion show had started. Lucienne would give a little talk and then the first
model was supposed to go out. Both Mom and
Lucienne would be up there giving the fashion
commentary. Neither one of them would be backstage until the show was over.

"Rosie?" Nicole sounded desperate.

"Nicole, can't you at least remember *something*
about the accessories?"

"Yes." She sniffed tearfully. "They all came in
plastic bags with little colored dots on them."

"Yeah, well, we got that far before," I said. "What do you want me to do?"

"You could do the accessorizing, Rosie," she said suddenly. "You're wonderful with accessories."

"Listen, maybe we'd better just tell the models—"

"*No!*" Nicole squealed. "After all the work your mom and everyone else has done, we can't have something like this ruin the whole show. It wouldn't be fair. Please, Rosie, I know you can do it."

Tanya was standing by the first rack talking to the twins. They kept looking back at Nicole and me.

"*Please*, Rosie. I'll take over what you were doing." I must have nodded, because Nicole went over to where I was supposed to stand to help the models change.

"Well, here goes nothing," I muttered to myself. I went to the rack where Nicole had put all the accessories. All the scarves were on hangers with absolutely no indication of what outfits they were to be worn with. The jewelry had been arranged on Cinderella's jewelry-display racks. It was beautiful stuff. But I had no idea what to do with any of it.

"Well," Tanya said. She was standing near the end of the rack. "I've got to go out now." She had on a pair of Lucienne silk harem pants with a white silk shirt. Her crimped hair swished around her shoulders.

I took a deep breath and grabbed a pair of gold hoop earrings and a wide gold cuff bracelet. "Put these on." I took the gorgeous silk patchwork jacket from the rack. "Here, toss this over your right shoulder and hook it casually on your finger."

Tanya looked skeptical, but did what I told her. Then she looked in the full-length mirror. "Anything you say." She smiled at her image and sailed out of the room. I could hear Mom introducing her. I was contemplating running out the back door when the twins came up dressed in summery-looking gauze miniskirts and matching shirts. One outfit was saffron, the other lime green.

I handed a huge black silk rose to the twin in green. "Pin this at your waist and put all those black bracelets on." I pushed her over to the rack where Nicole had put all the bracelets.

I grabbed two silk scarves—one bright yellow, the other reddish orange—and twisted them together. "Here, belt yourself, Mindy."

"I'm Meg," she said as she tied the scarves around her waist. "What jewelry?"

I dropped a gold chain loaded with dangling coins around her neck. "Here, there are earrings to match. Do you want the dangles or the big single coins?"

"Dangles," Meg said.

I lost track of time after that. We finished the first rack and pushed it to the other side of the room. Nicole hauled rack number two out. Tanya grabbed the red hanger and started to put on the outfit. "We go into suits now, then cocktail dresses," she said to me.

I had been doing fine because I didn't have time to think. All of a sudden there was a pause while Lucienne gave a plug for the children's hospital, and then I had the world's biggest anxiety attack. Nicole came over and offered me a soda, but I shook my head. I felt like I might throw up.

"You're doing a fantastic job," Nicole said, sounding awed. "You saved my life."

I gave her a weak grin.

"In fact, you really saved the show." She gave me a hug.

Nicole may have thought I saved the show, but I was afraid Lucienne might think I had ruined it. After all, a person with such an elaborate system for coordinating outfits was probably not too happy to see my improvisations. In fact, I was worried that she might come storming into the back room, demanding my head. But I didn't have time to give that any more thought because just then Zivia came out in a gorgeous suit with her red hair pulled back into an elegant knot.

The navy-blue business suit featured cuffed shorts rather than a skirt. I figured the accessories should be fairly conservative. So when Zivia made a turn and said, "What can we do for this?" I grabbed a pin I had admired earlier. It was a modern version of an old-fashioned lapel watch.

"Perfect." Zivia put it on, along with the small gold earrings I handed her, and sailed toward the door.

I sat down for a second and let out a long

breath. A top model thought that I had picked the perfect accessories!

Nicole was putting the first batch of clothes back on the rack. Suddenly I was dying of thirst. "Nicole, is there any more soda?"

"I'll get you one," she said. "You just keep doing what you're doing."

The cocktail dresses were easier. The lines were simple—but what color! I loved matching strands of brilliant wooden beads and huge, dangling shoulder-duster earrings with the screaming reds, hot pinks, and juicy greens.

When Zivia came out of the dressing room in a clinging black strapless sequined gown, I handed her the beautiful silk jacket and earrings of jet beads that cascaded down from huge faux rubies.

"Leave the jacket open," I said.

She laughed and said, "You act like you were born to this, Rosie."

I could feel a glow suffuse my whole body. I wouldn't have been surprised if somebody had shouted to turn off the light in the back room. I felt as if a spotlight had been turned on inside me. But I couldn't spend too much time basking in praise because Kiki was standing in front of me in the wedding gown, traditionally the last piece in a fashion show. She couldn't find her bouquet.

"I don't remember a bouquet," Nicole said.

"I can't go out there bare-handed," Kiki said.

The wedding gown was a very simple strapless white satin mini, worn with shoulder-length satin gloves and a pouf of tulle at the side of her head. Kiki was putting on the pearl drop earrings.

"Hurry, I'm on." She started for the door. I grabbed the yellow rose that Lucienne had given me and shoved it into Kiki's hand. She frowned at the lone flower.

"It's Lucienne's trademark," I said.

Kiki's face brightened and she went out the door.

The applause was thunderous at the end of the show. I went to the door and peeked out because I wanted to see where Allie, Becky, and Julie were sitting, but I also wanted to be able to run if I saw Lucienne coming toward me with fire in her eyes.

The models were mingling with all the people in the store. I saw Allie and her mother talking to Zivia and Julie's mother was looking at the bridal gown. Anyone who has three daughters had to be interested in stuff like that.

I caught Allie's eye and she started over to me just as Julie came running from the other side of the room. "Rosie, the models told us that you picked out all the accessories," she yelled. "They were incredible!"

"Completely," Allie said.

I pulled them into the back room with me.

"I hope so," I said. "The models said so, but I haven't talked to Mom or Lucienne yet." I explained to them how Nicole had mixed up all the accessories and how she'd asked me to step in.

Right then Becky came through the door holding a tray loaded with scrumptious-looking canapés. "Wasn't it fantastic?" she said. She held the tray out to me. "Mom and Russell are putting the food out now. I figured by the time you got out front, all the good stuff would be gone."

"Guess what? Rosie did all the accessories for the show." Julie reached for a cheese puff and offered it to me. "Here, you deserve the first one." Coming from Julie, the first puff was the ultimate compliment.

"I don't think I can get it down," I said. "Suddenly my throat is kind of dry."

"Rosie, you really were fantastic," Julie said. Allie and Becky nodded.

"You think I was fantastic, Julie, and the models seemed to think I was fantastic, and for a while, even I thought I was pretty good, but now I don't know. My stomach is full of dive-bombing butterflies."

"They probably came for the refreshments," Julie said. "Maybe if you feed them, they'll go away."

I was just putting the cheese puff in my mouth when I saw Mom coming through the door into the back room. Lucienne was right behind her.

I handed the cheese puff back to Julie. "I think maybe you should give me a blindfold and a cigarette."

"What?" Allie said. "Rosie, you don't smoke."

"I'll explain it to you," Julie began. Then she saw Mom and Lucienne, so she pulled Allie back and whispered, "Firing squad."

Mom must have heard Julie, because she looked at her with a faint smile and said, "Nothing quite so drastic, Julie." Then she turned to me. "But I'd like an explanation."

"It was my fault, Mrs. Torres," Nicole burst out before I could say a word. She started to tell Mom about the mix-up with the accessories when Lucienne broke through the circle and looked at me. I could hear my friends suck in their breath. I just stopped breathing altogether.

"The models told me who did the accessories." Lucienne stared at me for what seemed like two days before she added, "Brilliant."

I could hear a whoosh as Allie, Julie, and Becky started breathing again.

"Brilliant?" I said in a tiny voice. I could hardly believe my ears.

"Nothing short of it," she said warmly. "If I could, I would steal you away from your mother and take you on the rest of the tour with me."

If there were any reports of a flying saucer over Canfield that night, it wasn't an invasion of aliens—it was me, Rosie Torres, flying home from the fashion show. I'll bet my favorite jeans that my feet never touched the ground.

Ten

I knew my mother was really proud of me. Not only did she offer me a sip of the champagne that Dad brought to the store while we were cleaning up, she offered to let me sleep in the next morning. She said she would call the school and explain how I had stayed late at the store to help Lucienne and the models pack up.

I didn't think it would be fair for me to stay home, because Allie, Becky, and Julie had stayed to help, too. And besides, I couldn't sleep in because I wanted to get the morning paper as soon as it was delivered. There was going to be a review of the show in the paper. Mom said the fashion editor of the *Canfield Times* had been in the first row.

Mom was nervous about the review, too. She

almost dropped the can of coffee. I caught it just in time.

"I don't feel like sweeping coffee up again, Mom." I put the can on the table.

Mom nodded and went to the front door to see if the paper carrier had been there. She was gone for a few minutes before I heard her yell.

"Rosie, we did it!"

That "we" was like music. I ran to the front hall. Mom was standing there holding a section of the paper. The rest of the paper was on the floor at her feet.

"What does it say, Mom?"

"Listen." She cleared her throat. "'Yesterday's fashion show at Patricia Torres's shop, Cinderella, was a smashing success. Not only did Canfield get a close look at Lucienne's summer line, the Children's Research Center will be richer by many thousands of dollars.'"

"I forgot about the sales," I said.

"Everybody at the show had an order form," Mom said. "They turned them in to Lucienne before they left. She said her company will ship the clothes within two weeks." Mom laughed. "By then I should be just about rested up from the show."

Then Mom gave me a bear hug. "Rosie, I can't tell you how proud I was of you yesterday and how silly I was not to have you working on the show from day one. You are wonderfully creative. I want you to know that I'll try never to underestimate you again."

I read the rest of the review while Mom and Dad had breakfast. Most of it was about Lucienne's fabulous designs, but the very last part of the review was the best: "Clever accessories accented the clothes and showed the detail that one expects from one of the country's leading designers. Especially charming was the pairing of a glamorous silk patchwork jacket with harem pants and again with a sophisticated evening dress. The accessories showed the brilliance and audacity one could expect only from Lucienne."

When I read that line to my parents, both of them smiled. "Definitely a rave," Dad said. "At the risk of being mistaken for a maharajah I would like to take all the talented women who pulled off that job to dinner. That means you and Nicole."

"And your friends," my mom added.

"That's great, Dad. When?"

"Why not tonight? If you don't have a previous engagement, that is."

"I'll call and make reservations at the Moon-dance," Mom said. "I'll also call Nicole. Rosie, ask your friends and give me a call at the store."

I told my friends about dinner on the bus to school. They were thrilled—and available.

Before I went to the cafeteria for lunch, I called Mom at Cinderella.

"Rosie, I just saw Lucienne off," she told me. "She came to the house right after you left this morning. She was sorry not to be able to say goodbye to you in person, but she left you a note and invited us down to New York as soon as she finishes this tour."

I gasped. "That would be awesome, Mom. Can we go?"

"I don't see why not. We're headed that way this summer to see your grandmother. But let's take one treat at a time. Can the girls make it tonight?"

"Yep. What time shall I tell them?"

"Dad said he'd leave the office at six, so he'll

pick up Allie and Julie around six-fifteen and meet us at the Moondance. I'll be home about five."

I went into the cafeteria and joined Becky and Julie at our favorite table. Allie was just heading there with her tray.

"I can't wait to go to the Moondance for dinner," Julie said. "Becky, what's the special today?"

"Julie Berger," Allie said, "you're the only person I know who can get excited about dinner while eating lunch."

Julie laughed. "Lunch is just to keep my taste buds in training for dinner."

"I hope they're in shape," Becky said. "It's Italian night. When I left for school this morning, Russell was starting his sauce."

"That means there will be chicken parmigiana," I said, licking my lips. "That is my absolute, all-time favorite. Boy, a rave review this morning and a feast tonight—this is a great moment in history."

We spent the rest of the lunch period talking about what we were going to wear that night. I was really excited and planned to look extra special.

I told Allie and Julie that my dad would pick

them up about six-fifteen and that Mom and I would meet them about six-thirty at the Moondance.

"That's one advantage of living where I do," Becky said. "I only have to walk downstairs. In a couple of months I'll have to walk all the way across the yard."

The bell rang and we all gathered our trays and started out of the cafeteria.

"Well, onward to Appomattox," Julie said. The battle at Appomattox was what we'd be covering in history next period.

Wouldn't you know Casey Wyatt would step up right behind Julie? "Hey, Berger."

Julie turned around and the rest of us stopped and waited to see what Casey wanted to say to her.

"I heard that Lee wanted to surrender directly to Lincoln, but he couldn't remember his Gettysburg address."

The whole Party Line groaned but then Allie giggled and the rest of us broke down and laughed all the way to history class.

When I got home from school I spotted an envelope propped on the hall table. It was addressed to me. I opened it and found a copy of the review. The last line was circled and Lucienne had replaced her name with mine. It was signed, "With much gratitude and respect, Lucienne." I couldn't have asked for a better souvenir of the fashion show.

I danced up the stairs and opened my bedroom door. There on my bed was a garment bag with the yellow rose logo. I almost broke the zipper opening it. I pulled out of the bag the most beautiful piece of clothing in the entire world— the silk patchwork jacket. I stared at it in astonishment.

Suddenly I knew exactly what I was wearing to dinner.

SPECIAL PARTY TIP

Rosie's Tip on Decorating Your Own T-shirt

T-shirt decorating is a lot of fun for T-shirt lovers of any age. All it takes is a T-shirt, fabric glue, and any materials that strike your fancy. I recommend fabric paints, ribbons, buttons, glitter, sequins and lace. Just put out all your supplies on a table and go wild!

A great way to apply paint is with sponge cutouts. Use a cookie cutter and trace the shape onto a sponge, preferably a thin one. Cut it out with scissors and you're all set. You just dip the sponge into a saucer of paint and stamp it lightly but firmly on the fabric. It's a great way to make perfect hearts, stars, and animal shapes, even if you aren't good at drawing.

These techniques can also be used on other kinds of clothing, such as socks, jeans, sneakers, headbands—just about anything you can think of. Have fun!

One day Allie, Rosie, Becky and Julie saved a birthday party from becoming a complete disaster. The next day, the four best friends are running their own business...

The Party Line ®

by Carrie Austen

___#1: ALLIE'S WILD SURPRISE   0-425-12047-3/$2.75

___#2: JULIE'S BOY PROBLEM   0-425-12048-1/$2.75

___#3: BECKY'S SUPER SECRET   0-425-12131-3/$2.75

___#4: ROSIE'S POPULARITY PLAN   0-425-12169-0/$2.75

___#5: ALLIE'S BIG BREAK   0-425-12266-2/$2.75

___#6: JULIE'S DREAM DATE   0-425-12301-4/$2.75

___#7: BECKY BARTLETT,   0-425-12348-0/$ 2.75
       SUPERSTAR

___#8: ROSIE'S MYSTERY ON ICE   0-425-12440-1/$2.75

* A General Licensing Company Book